Make a Pencil Holder from a Paper Cup

Jonathon Phillips
Photographs by Lindsay Edwards

Contents

Teacher's Note

Have a selection of recycled paper cups ready for students. Most paper cups contain some plastic, so they cannot be put into recycling bins. Several waste collection agencies collect and recycle only these paper cups. They can provide you with the paper cups required for this procedure. Ensure you wash the cups in warm, soapy water before giving them to your students.

Goal

To make a pencil holder from a **recycled** paper cup

Materials

You will need:

- a recycled paper cup
- a pencil
- scissors

- a ball of blue wool

- a ball of white wool

- a ball of green wool

- measuring tape.

Steps

1. Make nine marks around the top of your paper cup with the pencil.

   The spaces between the marks must be even.

2. With the scissors, start at each mark and cut down to the bottom of the cup.

   You now have nine **warps**.

   The warps are what you will **weave** the wool through to make your **pattern**.

3. With the scissors, cut one string from each ball of wool. Each string should be about 80 centimetres long.

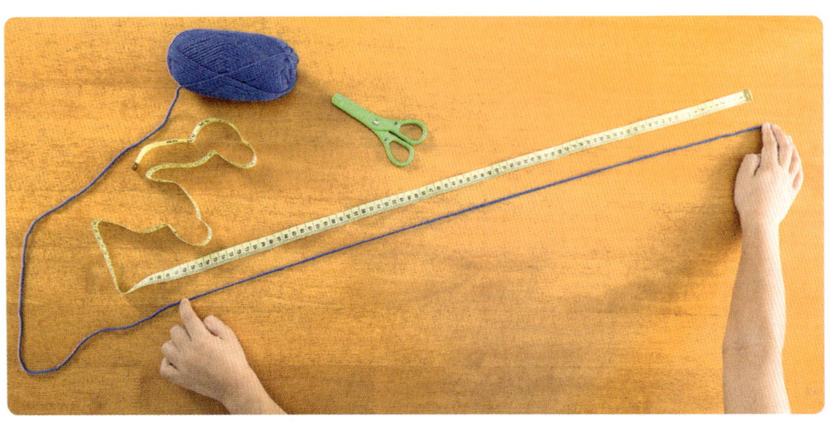

4. Take the string of blue wool. Tie it around one of the warps, at the bottom of the cup.

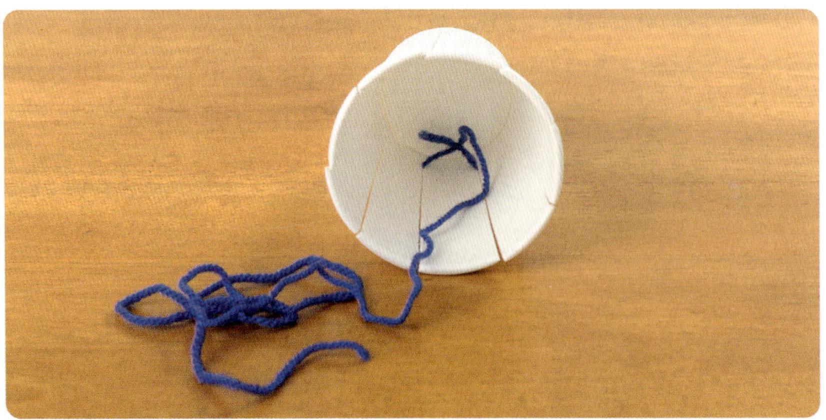

If you need help to tie the knot,
ask your teacher.

Look to see that the knot
is on the inside of the cup.
The knot should not be seen
when the pencil holder is done.

5. Start to weave the wool around the cup. Pull the wool in between the warps, going in and out.

Don't pull the wool too hard, as this will bend your cup.

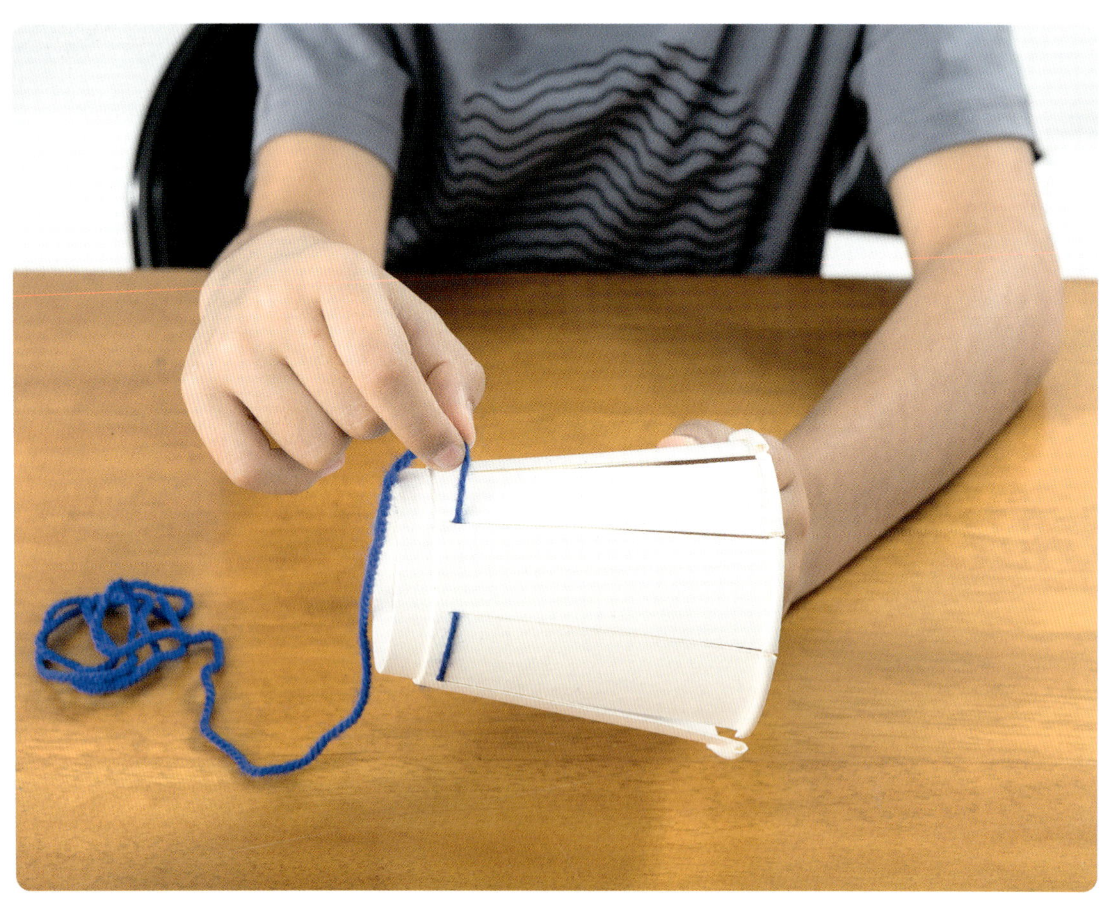

6. The woven wool should not be too loose. Every so often, stop weaving and push the wool down towards the bottom of the cup.

7. When you are nearly at the end of the blue wool, take the string of white wool.
Tie the two strings of wool together.

Once again, look to see that the knot is on the inside of the cup.

8. Follow steps 5 and 6 again.

Then, do the same with the string of green wool.

9. To make a pattern, begin weaving again with another string of blue wool.

10. Keep on weaving with your three balls of wool. Stop weaving when the wool is at the top of the paper cup.

11. Tie the end of the last string of wool around a warp.

With the scissors, poke the ends of the knot behind the woven wool inside the cup, so the ends will not be seen.

Now, you have a pencil holder that will last you a long time!

Put your favourite pencils and pens into your pencil holder.

Glossary

pattern *(noun)* lines or shapes that are done over and over, or repeated

recycled *(adjective)* when something old has been made into something new

warps *(noun)* bits of the cup that have been cut so the wool can be pulled between them

weave *(verb)* to make a pattern with strings of wool by pulling them in between the warps, so they cross over

Make a Pencil Holder from a Paper Cup

Text: Jonathon Phillips
Publisher: Eliza Webb
Editor: Jarrah Moore
Project editor: Jarrah Moore
Project designer: James Steer
Designer: MAPG
Photographs: Lindsay Edwards
Props: Vaughan Duck
Production controller: Alice Kane
Reprint: Siew Han Ong

Acknowledgements
Back cover (background pattern): Shutterstock.com/sahua d.

PM Guided Reading
Turquoise Level 17

When the Volcano Erupted
Ivy's Great Big, Beautiful Hat
Why Frogs Croak
A Day with No Internet!
Nelson, the Baby Elephant
Toby and the Accident
Little Dinosaur Escapes
Rescuing Nelson
Number Plates
Animal Builders
The Surf Wave Lagoon
Make a Pencil Holder from a Paper Cup

ISBN 978 0 17 032848 7

Cengage Learning Australia
Level 5 , 80 Dorcas Street
Southbank VIC 3006
Phone: 1300 790 853
Email: aust.nelsonprimary@cengage.com

For learning solutions, visit cengage.com.au

Printed in China by 1010 Printing International Ltd
2 3 4 5 6 7 26

This product is made from materials that are compliant
with the EU Deforestation Regulation

PM

1
2
3
4
5
6
7
8
9
10
11
12
13
14
15
16
17
18
19
20
21
22
23
24
25
26
27
28
29
30

Find out how to make a pencil holder from a recycled paper cup! With a paper cup and some wool, you can make a pencil holder that will last you a long time.

Procedure

ISBN 978-0170328487
9 780170 328487

Lev
1

NELSON
A Cengage Company

Our Five Senses

Sarah Russell

Our Five Senses

Level 15

Running Words 272 **Text Type** Information Report (Informative)

Curriculum Area Science

Retelling to encourage critical thinking about the content

Ask each student to retell the information report in his or her own words. Record the retelling for further discussion and reflection.

Questions to reinforce meaning and stimulate discussion

Literal

1 What are our five senses?

2 Why do we need our senses?

3 What can we hear when it rains?

4 How does our skin feel if we are out in the sun too long?

Inferential

5 How do we know if it is safe to cross the road?

6 How do we know if there is a fire?

7 How do our tongues help stop us from getting sick?

Links with other PM Guided Reading Books and Cards

Level 15	Card	Narrative	*Liam's Tooth*
Level 15	Book	Poetry	*The World Around Me*
Level 16	Book	Information Report	*Windy Days*